Dear Parent:
Your child's love of reading starts here!

Every child learns to read in a different way and at his or her own speed. Some go back and forth between reading levels and read favorite books again and again. Others read through each level in order. You can help your young reader improve and become more confident by encouraging his or her own interests and abilities. From books your child reads with you to the first books he or she reads alone, there are I Can Read Books for every stage of reading:

SHARED READING
Basic language, word repetition, and whimsical illustrations, ideal for sharing with your emergent reader

BEGINNING READING
Short sentences, familiar words, and simple concepts for children eager to read on their own

READING WITH HELP
Engaging stories, longer sentences, and language play for developing readers

READING ALONE
Complex plots, challenging vocabulary, and high-interest topics for the independent reader

ADVANCED READING
Short paragraphs, chapters, and exciting themes for the perfect bridge to chapter books

I Can Read Books have introduced children to the joy of reading since 1957. Featuring award-winning authors and illustrators and a fabulous cast of beloved characters, I Can Read Books set the standard for beginning readers.

A lifetime of discovery begins with the magical words "I Can Read!"

Visit www.icanread.com for information
on enriching your child's reading experience.

For Frances's friends everywhere

HarperCollins®, ≝®, and I Can Read Book® are trademarks of HarperCollins Publishers.

Library of Congress Cataloging-in-Publication Data is available.
ISBN 978-0-06-083801-0 (trade bdg.)—ISBN 978-0-06-083803-4 (pbk.)

❖

First Edition

I Can Read!™

READING
2
WITH HELP

BEST FRIENDS FOR FRANCES

by Russell Hoban

Pictures by Lillian Hoban

HarperCollinsPublishers

It was a fine summer morning,

so Frances took out her bat and ball.

"Will you play ball with me?"

said her little sister, Gloria.

"No," said Frances.

"You are too little."

Gloria sat down and cried.

Frances walked over to her friend

Albert's house, singing a song:

Sisters that are much too small

To throw or catch or bat a ball

Are really not much good at all,

Except for crying.

When Frances got to Albert's house,

he was coming out with

a large brown paper bag.

"Let's play baseball," said Frances.

"I can't," said Albert.

"Today is my wandering day."

"Where do you wander?" said Frances.

"I just go around until I get hungry,"

said Albert. "Then I eat my lunch."

"That's a big lunch," said Frances.

"It's only four or five sandwiches,"
said Albert, "and apples, bananas,
cupcakes, and some chocolate milk."

"Can I wander, too?" said Frances.

"No," said Albert.

"You can't do the things I do
on my wandering days."

"Like what?" said Frances.

"Snake and frog work," said Albert.

"Throwing stones at fences.
Looking for crow feathers."

"I can do all that," said Frances,
"except the snake and frog work."

"That's what I mean," said Albert.

"I'd have to ruin the whole day,
showing you how."

Then Albert went off to wander.

And Frances walked home slowly,

singing:

Fat boys that eat too much lunch

Can't do a thing but munch and crunch

And play with snakes and frogs.

When Frances got home, Gloria said,

"Will you play ball with me now?"

"You can't bat

and you can't catch," said Frances.

"I can if you stand close," said Gloria.

"All right," said Frances,

and she played ball with Gloria.

15

The next morning,

Frances went to Albert's house.

Albert was playing ball with Harold.

"Can I play?" said Frances.

"She's not much good,"

said Harold to Albert, "and besides,

this is a no-girls game."

16

"All right," said Frances.

"Then I will go home and play

a no-boys game with Gloria,

Mr. Fat Albert. So ha, ha, ha."

Frances walked home,

and as she walked she sang:

Boys to throw and catch and bat

Are all the friends that Mr. Fat

Albert will have from now on.

He will not have me.

When Frances got home,

Gloria said,

"How did you play so fast?"

"It was a fast game," said Frances.

"You're lucky that you have

a friend to play with," said Gloria.

"I wish I had a friend."

"I thought Ida was your friend,"

said Frances.

"Ida is away at camp," said Gloria,

"and she only plays dolls.

She never wants to catch frogs."

"Can you catch frogs?" said Frances.

"Yes," said Gloria.

"I can show you."

"Later," said Frances.

"Do you want to play ball?"

"All right," said Gloria.

"If any boys come, they can't play,"

said Frances,

"and I think I will

be your friend now."

"How can a sister be a friend?"
said Gloria.

"You'll see," said Frances.

"For frogs and ball and dolls?"

"Yes," said Frances.

"And will you show me how
to print my name?" said Gloria.

"Yes," said Frances.

"Then you will be my best friend,"
said Gloria.

"Will it just be today, or longer?"

"Longer," said Frances.

"And today we will have a picnic.

"There will be songs and games

and prizes.

And no boys," said Frances.

Mother helped Frances and Gloria

get everything ready and packed

in Frances's wagon.

Frances and Gloria set off.

In the wagon were

a picnic lunch in a hamper,

two burlap sacks for the sack race,

an egg for the egg toss,

and a jar with two frogs

for the frog-jumping contest.

Frances made a sign that said:

BEST FRIENDS

OUTING

NO BOYS

They held the sign and Frances sang:

When best friends have an outing,

There are jolly times in store.

There are games and there are prizes,

There is also something more.

There is something in a hamper

That is very good to eat.

When best friends have an outing,

It's a very special treat,

With no boys.

Frances and Gloria

passed Albert's house.

"What's in the hamper?" said Albert,

running out of his house.

"I don't know," said Frances.

"Nothing much.

Hard-boiled eggs and fresh tomatoes.

Carrot and celery sticks.

Some cream cheese-and-jelly

sandwiches, I think.

Salami, pepper-and-egg sandwiches.

Ice-cold root beer, watermelon and

strawberries and cream for dessert.

"There are salt and pepper shakers
and napkins and a checked tablecloth,
which is the way girls do it."
"Could I come along
on the eating?" said Albert.
"You mean outing," said Frances.

"That wagon looks heavy to pull,"
said Albert. "You will get tired
unless I help you."

"I don't know," said Frances.

"You can see from the sign
that this is a no-boys outing.
And it is only for best friends."

"What good is an outing
without boys?" said Albert.

"It is just as good as a ball game
without girls," said Frances,
"and maybe a whole lot better."

"Can I be a best friend?" said Albert.

"I don't think it is the kind of thing
you can do," said Frances.
"And it would ruin my whole day
to have to show you."
"I can do it," said Gloria.
"I can be a best friend,
and I can catch frogs, too."

30

"I can catch frogs *and* snakes,"

said Albert.

"Let him be a best friend,"

said Gloria.

"And he can show me

how to catch snakes."

"I'll get my snake pillowcase

right now," said Albert.

"Well, I'm not sure," said Frances.

"Maybe you'll be best friends

when it's lunch-in-the-hamper time.

But how about when it's

no-girls-baseball time?"

"When we are best friends,
there won't be no-girls baseball,"
said Albert.
"All right," said Frances.
She crossed out the NO BOYS
on the sign.
Then they started off again.

Albert pulled the wagon,
and Frances and Gloria
carried the sign.
The outing place was at the tree
on the hill by the pond.

First, Albert caught

a snake for Gloria,

and then they played games.

Gloria won the sack race.

Frances won the egg toss.

Albert won the frog-jumping contest

with a fresh frog from the pond.

So everybody won a prize.

Then Frances made up a party song.

And everybody sang it.

When the wasps and the bumblebees

Have a party,

Nobody comes that can't buzz.

When the chicks and ducklings

Have an outing,

Everyone has to wear fuzz.

When the frog and the snake

Have their yearly clambake,

There's plenty

Of wiggling and hopping.

They splash in the pond

And the marshes beyond,

And everyone has to get sopping.

"And at the Best Friends Outing,"
said Albert,
"everyone has to eat, don't they?"
"Yes," said Frances and Gloria.
They opened the hamper.
"I'm not sure we can eat it all,"
said Frances.

"That is what best friends are for,"
said Albert.

And he gave Frances and Gloria a ride
in the wagon, all the way home.

The next day, Albert came over
with a bunch of daisies for Frances.
"What are the daisies for?" she said.
"Well, we are best friends now,
and I am a boy," said Albert.
"That makes me your best boyfriend.
So that is why I brought you daisies."
"Thank you," said Frances.

Then Gloria sat down

on the steps and cried.

"Why are you crying?" said Frances.

"Now you have Albert

to be your best friend," said Gloria.

"And you won't be mine anymore."

"Yes, I will," said Frances.

"And I will give you half the daisies

Albert gave me."

So Frances gave Gloria
half the daisies,
and Gloria stopped crying.

Then Harold came over,

and everybody played baseball—

Gloria too.

About Frances

I'm so glad to see that so many children like
the Frances books, because I had a lot of fun
writing them. I got the idea for the first one,
Bedtime for Frances, from the little girl next
door who kept finding excuses for not going to
bed. After that I began all of my titles with B,
for luck. I liked making up the Frances songs.

> *Here's a little reading song,*
> *Singing it will not take long.*
> *Books are cozy, books are fun.*
> *Now my reading song is done.*

Russell Hoban

February 2008